Dear Parents:

Congratulations! Your child is taking the first steps on an exciting journey. The destination? Independent reading!

STEP INTO READING® will help your child get there. The program offers five steps to reading success. Each step includes fun stories and colorful art or photographs. In addition to original fiction and books with favorite characters, there are Step into Reading Non-Fiction Readers, Phonics Readers and Boxed Sets, Sticker Readers, and Comic Readers—a complete literacy program with something to interest every child.

Learning to Read, Step by Step!

Ready to Read   Preschool–Kindergarten
• big type and easy words • rhyme and rhythm • picture clues
For children who know the alphabet and are eager to begin reading.

Reading with Help   Preschool–Grade 1
• basic vocabulary • short sentences • simple stories
For children who recognize familiar words and sound out new words with help.

Reading on Your Own   Grades 1–3
• engaging characters • easy-to-follow plots • popular topics
For children who are ready to read on their own.

Reading Paragraphs   Grades 2–3
• challenging vocabulary • short paragraphs • exciting stories
For newly independent readers who read simple sentences with confidence.

Ready for Chapters   Grades 2–4
• chapters • longer paragraphs • full-color art
For children who want to take the plunge into chapter books but still like colorful pictures.

STEP INTO READING® is designed to give every child a successful reading experience. The grade levels are only guides; children will progress through the steps at their own speed, developing confidence in their reading. The F&P Text Level on the back cover serves as another tool to help you choose the right book for your child.

Remember, a lifetime love of reading starts with a single step!

For little brothers everywhere
—C.H. and E.T.

For Dave: the messiest person I know
—D.P.

Text copyright © 2005 by Cathy Hapka and Ellen Titlebaum.
Cover art and interior illustrations copyright © 2005 by Debbie Palen.

All rights reserved. Published in the United States by Random House Children's Books, a division of Penguin Random House LLC, New York.

Step into Reading, Random House, and the Random House colophon are registered trademarks of Penguin Random House LLC.

Visit us on the Web!
StepIntoReading.com
randomhousekids.com

Educators and librarians, for a variety of teaching tools, visit us at
RHTeachersLibrarians.com

Library of Congress Cataloging-in-Publication Data
Hapka, Cathy.
How not to babysit your brother / by Cathy Hapka and Ellen Titlebaum ; illustrated by Debbie Palen. — 1st ed.
    p. cm. — (Step into reading. Step 4 book)
Summary: When Grandma falls asleep, Will finds himself responsible for his little brother, Steve, and discovers the hard way what not to do when in charge.
ISBN 978-0-375-82856-0 (trade) — ISBN 978-0-375-92856-7 (lib. bdg.)
[1. Brothers—Fiction. 2. Babysitters—Fiction.] I. Titlebaum, Ellen. II. Palen, Debbie, ill. III. Title. IV. Series. PZ7 .H1996Ho 2005 [Fic]—dc22 2004003802

Printed in the United States of America First Edition 25 24 23 22 21 20 19

This book has been officially leveled by using the F&P Text Level Gradient™ Leveling System.

How **Not** to Babysit Your Brother

by Cathy Hapka and Ellen Titlebaum

illustrated by Debbie Palen

Random House 🏠 New York

Little Brothers Are Trouble

Hi, my name is Will.

I live with my parents, my grandma, my dog, Buster, and my little brother, Steve.

Steve is trouble. He's loud, he's smelly, and he's always around. If you have a little brother, you know *exactly* what I mean.

Last week, I found out just how much trouble he could be. That's when I learned how NOT to babysit my brother.

It all started when Mom went shopping.

Dad was out playing golf.

I was playing my new video game, Cowboy Stampede. I was about to reach Level 5. Usually my cowboy got trampled on Level 3.

"Bye, Mom," I said.

"Bye, Mom!" Steve sang out. He likes to copy everything I do.

"We'll be fine," Grandma told Mom. "Don't worry."

After Mom left, I went back to my game. Suddenly I felt a tug on my arm. "Can I play?"

It was Steve, of course.

"Go away," I said.

But it was too late. The cow trampled my cowboy. Two words came on the screen:

GAME OVER.

"Look what you did, twerp-head!" I said.

"Play nice, boys," Grandma said. She yawned and picked up a book.

I went back to my game. A minute later, I heard a snore.

I looked over at the couch. Grandma's book was on her lap and her eyes were closed.

"Grandma?" I said.

The only answer was another snore. She was fast asleep.

A Very Bad Idea

I looked over at Steve. He stared back at me.

"I'm bored," Steve said. "If Grandma's asleep, you have to babysit me. I want to play hide-and-seek."

"Okay," I said. "You hide first. One, two, three . . ."

I smiled as Steve ran out of the room. Buster ran after him. Steve loves hide-and-seek. I love my video game. Now we were both happy.

I waited until Steve and Buster were out of sight. Then I stopped counting and went back to my video game.

I didn't think about Steve again until
my cowboy was out of lasso points. Then
I realized that the house was very quiet.

Too quiet.

I turned away from the game and
looked at Grandma. She was still sleeping.

"Uh-oh," I said.

I went to find Steve. I looked for him under the stairs. I looked in the hall closet. Steve wasn't there.

This is when I learned Babysitting Lesson #1: When you're babysitting your brother, DON'T forget about him!

I continued to search. I checked under Steve's bed. Then I checked under my bed. I searched the basement, the garage, and my closet. There was no sign of Steve.

This was going to be harder than I thought. Where was Steve hiding?

CRASH!

Uh-oh, I thought.

I heard Buster barking in the kitchen. I ran to see what was going on.

A Very Big Mess

When I got there, the dog food bin was tipped over. Steve's head and shoulders were sticking out of the top. Dog food was stuck in his hair, on his clothes, and up his nose. He looked like an alien from the planet Yuck. He giggled as Buster licked some crumbs off his ear.

"What took you so long?" Steve asked when he saw me. A chunk of dog food flew out of his mouth.

Babysitting Lesson #2: When babysitting your brother, DON'T let him hide first!

"Get out of there," I told Steve. "We have to clean up this mess!"

Steve climbed out of the bin. "Why?" he asked. "Buster's cleaning it up."

"If Buster eats all this food, he'll get a stomach ache," I told him.

I wiped off the counter and swept the floor. But Steve was still covered in dog food and dog slobber.

"Come on, Steve," I said. "Let's go upstairs."

"Why?" Steve asked. He gave me an I-don't-trust-you look. "What's upstairs?"

"The bathtub," I said, grinning.

Steve hates baths.

I dragged Steve up to the bathroom.

"No bath!" he yelled.

"I'll give you a cookie," I said.

"NO BATH!"

We glared at each other. I had to think of something fast.

"If you take a bath," I said, "we'll play a game."

"What game?" Steve asked.

"It's called—TIDAL WAVE!"

"Tidal wave?" Steve said happily. "Okay!"

Babysitting Lesson #3: When your brother likes one of your ideas, be very, VERY worried!

Another Very, Very Bad Idea

Steve dragged his arms through the tub. "Danger! Danger!" he shouted. "TIDAL WAVE!"

Water washed over me.

"Hey!" I yelled.

Steve laughed. "Here comes another one!"

I was beginning to realize that Tidal Wave was a very, very bad idea.

"Stop!" I pleaded. "No more tidal waves!"

It was too late. Another wave came splashing out of the tub. This time Steve managed to soak me, all the stuff on the counter by the sink, and all four walls. Buster pushed the door open to see what we were doing. He got soaked, too.

Babysitting Lesson #4: NEVER let your little brother play Tidal Wave in the bathtub!

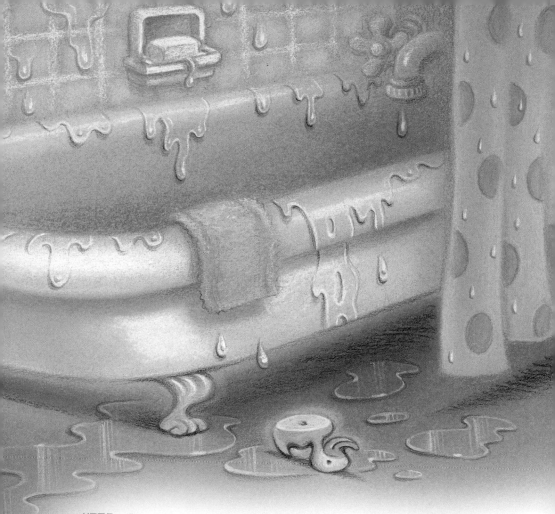

"We have to clean up before Grandma wakes up," I said.

Steve shrugged. "You can clean," he said.

"No," I said. "You're going to help me."

I gave Steve a towel. "I'll get a mop," I said. "Dry yourself off and don't make a bigger mess while I'm gone."

"Look," Steve said proudly when I came back with the mop. "Now the bathroom is EXTRA clean. And it sparkles!"

I groaned. There was toothpaste on the toilet seat. There was shaving cream on the sink. There was bubble bath dripping from the towel rack. Little wads of wet toilet paper were clinging to the walls. I could smell Mom's perfume, Dad's aftershave, and Grandma's lavender powder mixing together.

Babysitting Lesson #5: When babysitting your brother, don't let him out of your sight for even ONE MINUTE!

"All that cleaning made me hungry," Steve said. "I want a snack."

"Go straight to the kitchen," I croaked. "Do not wake Grandma. Do not hide. Do not pass GO. Do you understand me?"

Steve smiled his most innocent smile. "Sure. I'll make a snack for you, too." He hurried out of the bathroom, leaving a trail of water behind him.

My toothbrush was floating in the toilet. I fished it out and threw it away.

This was NOT how I wanted to spend Saturday afternoon!

Another Sticky, Smelly, Horrible Mess

After the bathroom was clean, I walked down to the kitchen. I gasped.

The refrigerator door was wide open. Steve was standing at the counter. A huge, half-made sandwich was in front of him— at least, I THINK it was a sandwich. It was made out of ham, a whole tomato, an entire cucumber, cold spaghetti, pickles, chocolate syrup, sardines, and yogurt.

Buster was licking a big blob of yogurt off the floor. Buster was having a very good day. So was Steve.

I was NOT having a good day.

Babysitting Lesson #6: When babysitting your brother, DON'T forget Babysitting Lesson #5—if you do, you'll regret it every time!

Steve took a big bite of his sandwich.

"Yuck!" he cried. "This tastes gross. Do you want it, Will?"

He shoved the sandwich across the counter. I tried to catch it, but I was too slow.

The sandwich landed on the floor with
a SPLAT!

"Uh-oh," Steve said. "Messy. Should I
clean it up, Will?"

"No!" I cried. "I'll do it. Just stay out of
the way."

I cleaned the kitchen for the second time. Then I went to the family room. Grandma was still asleep on the couch. But now she had a weird streak of sparkly pink stuff on her nose. Steve was sitting next to her.

"What are you doing?" I hissed. "You'll wake her up!"

"Shh," Steve replied. He held up Mom's makeup bag. "I'm just making her look pretty."

I watched in horror as he pulled out a lipstick and some face powder.

"Quit that!" I whispered.

I grabbed the makeup and the bag and shoved it all under the couch.

I took a tissue and gently wiped most of the makeup from Grandma's hair and face. Then I looked at Steve. He had smudges of red lipstick all over his face, and his arms were dusted with sparkling powder.

Why, oh *why*, did I forget Babysitting Lesson #5?

"You're a mess," I said.

"Time for more Tidal Wave?" Steve asked hopefully.

I shuddered and shook my head. Then I did what I should have done all along. I let Steve play Cowboy Stampede while I went to get a washcloth.

All's Well That Ends Well . . . or Is It?

When Mom walked in, Steve was still playing with my video game. I was reading a magazine. I was too tired to do anything else. At least Steve was clean. It took an hour to scrub the makeup off of him.

"Hello, everyone," Mom said with a smile. "Looks like things were quiet while I was gone."

Grandma's eyelids fluttered. "Oh, my," she said. "That was a nice rest."

"Were the boys good?" Mom asked her.

"Oh, yes," Grandma said. "I hardly heard a peep out of them all afternoon."

"Will was my babysitter," Steve cried happily. "I helped him clean!"

Mom was staring curiously at Grandma. I gulped as I noticed that Grandma still had a patch of glittery face powder on her chin.

Just then, Buster walked in.

Mom stared at the dog. Then she stared at me.

"Well?" she asked sternly.

I grinned weakly. "It's a long story. . . ."

Babysitting Lesson #7: When babysitting your brother, DON'T forget to clean up the dog!